D1103779

WRITTEN BY

GABE SORIA

ILLUSTRATED BY

RAFA RIBS

VINCENT BATIGNOLE

COLORS BY

WARREN WUCINICH

Bright Family created by Matthew Cody and Derick Brooks

Andrews McMeel Publishing
a division of Andrews McMeel Universal
1130 Walnut Street, Kansas City, Missouri 64106

www.andrewsmcmeel.com

Epic! Creations, Inc.
702 Marshall Street, Suite 280
Redwood City, California 94063

www.getepic.com

23 24 25 26 27 SDB 10 9 8 7 6 5 4 3 2 1

Paperback ISBN: 978-1-5248-7868-9
Hardback ISBN: 978-1-5248-7869-6

Library of Congress Control Number: 2022943706

Design by Dan Nordskog and Carolyn Bahar

Made by:
RR Donnelley (Guangdong) Printing Solutions Company Ltd.
Address and location of manufacturer:
No. 2, Minzhu Road, Daning, Humen Town,
Dongguan City, Guangdong Province, China 523930
1st Printing – 11/14/22

FOR RED BOOTS AND NACHO.
G. S.

TO MY MOM, NEUSA, FOR ALWAYS
BEING SO SUPPORTIVE.
R. R.

TO MY DEAR SERENA VALENTINO.
YOU WERE THE FIRST TO BELIEVE
IN ME, AND I'LL BE FOREVER
GRATEFUL FOR ALL THE LOVE,
THE SUPPORT, AND THE MAGICAL
THOUGHTS YOU ALWAYS
SEND MY WAY.
V. B.

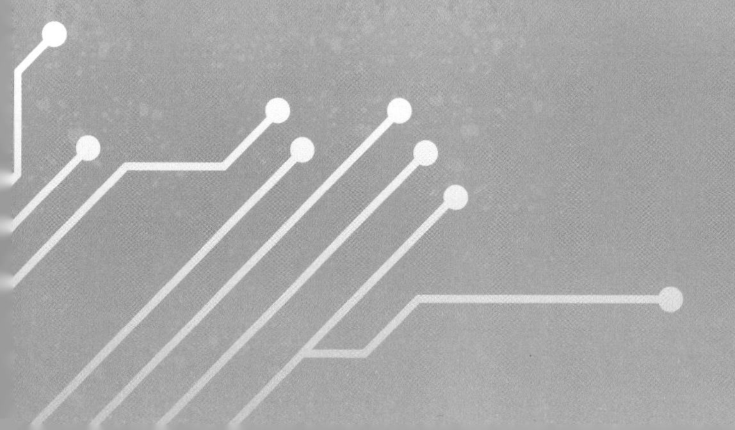

CHAPTER 1
A BRIGHT FAMILY VACATION

Do you need any help with that ***containment unit,*** Nia?
I'm pretty busy over here, but I can spare a moment to recalibrate its settings.
I'm ***fine,*** Mom! You just do ***you!***
Okay--I just need a few more minutes to equalize the pressure on either side of this portal before I send these creatures back to their home.
If I don't... boom!

Boom?

Biiig boom.

Okay, I'll keep these little guys off your back. They're just sea babies in a confusing new world.
BONK
You sure you don't need my help?

Mom, I've got this!
Okay, okay! I wonder how your dad and brother are doing on the surface...
Jayden?

Meanwhile, on the shore...
This...is...the...greatest!
Jayden, please stop horsing around.
This is supposed to be a simple containment and closure operation.
Relax, Dad--you worry too much.
Whoa!
It's not worry, Jayden--it's probability analysis!
Be careful with her--it's not her fault she slipped through that portal.
Yeah, Mom. It's Dad's fault, right?
Well...kind of? Not really... maybe a little.
Hey! I heard that, Banira!
BEEP
BEEP
What's that?

I've got another call. It's my dad *again.*

I'll send him to voice mail.
Jayden, hold on until I finish this perimeter fence...
...now!

BONK
Oof!

Are you okay?
Yup. Good thing this sand is so soft!
It's like a feather bed made of super tiny *rocks.*

The water's, like, the *perfect* temperature.
Okay, I'm almost ready. Pressure's equalized!

On top of closing the portal, this will also return everything from the other side to its place of origin. In 3...2...1...

Whoa.

Whoa.

This kinda reminds me of the time we buried our goldfish Mr. Fins...
SHWIRL
Don't worry, honey. Those sea serpents are going to be fine.

It worked! They're back on their side of the closed portal!

Way to go!
Well done, you two. But Jayden and Nia, you both took some *very* unnecessary risks.
As it expressly states i the Bright Family Safet Protocols, Chapter 8, Section 6--

Hush, Mr. Safety Police. Enjoy the moment.
But--

But nothing. Well done, everyone.
That was the *last* portal we had to close, and we couldn' have done it if we hadn't tackled it as a *family.*

This is nice, isn't it? So relaxing.
Yeahhhhhh...
The job is *technically* done, but I still have a *lot* of data to analyz back in my lab...
Chill out, dear.
Ahem. Pardon me!

As Lord High Manager of the Moon of Grabar location of Galactic Resorts and Spas...
...I would like to be the st to welcome you to our ablishment and extend our atitude for taking care of that pesky sea serpent problem. Thank you!
Who the what now?
Oh, well, don't know if ou should be *hanking* us...
You're very welcome, Lord High Manager...?
Fleuben! At your service.
Resorts and Spas?
Benjamin, take it from someone who's saved the world a few times...
When meone thanks ou, just say *'re welcome.* explanations.
Yes, dear.
And as a token of our thanks, I, on behalf of the Management Cloud Intelligence, would like to offer the Bright Family an all-expenses-paid stay here at the resort! No charge!
e couldn't. Accepting yment for doing what we do just doesn't seem right.
It's time I got back to my laboratory!
And Jayden and I need to get back to school!
Leave me out of this, Nia.

Are you **sure?** Why don't I give you a **tour** before you decide?

You've already seen our **gold sand** beach, but did you know that we've terraformed our coastline so the waves are guaranteed to be **perfect?**
Plus, the water is always the **ideal** temperature!

And have you seen the **culinarium,** our gourmet restaurant? It's open 25 hours a day, 8 days a week!
Dulce de leche fountain!
Space ramen!
Roast beast!
Vegetarian roast beast!
Chef Vril Taxus--he's famous!

There's also a mega **water park,** yo!

We've even got a **deluxe conference room** where scientists on vacation give lectures--when they're not getting relaxing massages, that is!
Vacation Scientific Lectures:
The New Paradigm

Perfect surf...
Gourmet restaurant...
Water park, yo...
Vacation lectures...

o what do you say, Bright Family?
We have to discuss this among ourselves.

Huddle up, Bright Family!

he portal echnology s working well now.
I can definitely keep up with schoolwork here.
And we *could* use a little break.
Bring on the waterslides, man.
Okay, then. It's decided. Break!

leuben--we accept!
e have to ortal home o pack and ake care of ome things, o...see you omorrow?
Absolutely no problem. Your rooms will be ready when you arrive.

Let's go, portal-hoppers! Next stop: **home!**
Hey--where's **Dusty?**
There he is!
Dusty, you look great!
Yeah you do!
He was enjoying our **full-servic** robot spa while you dealt with th sea serpents. Did I mention the full-service robot spa?
Great place you've got here, Fleuben. We'll be back!
We look forward to your return!

I'm going to start packing!
Me too!
Yawn I cannot *wait* to sleep in a deluxe bed.
I think we need to do a quick review of the Bright Family Safety Protocols.

Gee whiz, it's my dad *again.*
I'll call him back later.
BEEP
BEEP

Benjamin Bright, don't you dare! You can take a break for a minute and talk to your father.
Okaaaaay. Hey, Dad! What's up?
Son! I've been calling you. Where ya been?

ell, you know-- usy times over ere. It's a long story.
'm sure it Does that nean you *forgot?*
Forgot what?
DING
DONG

There's someone at the door!
I'll get it!
Oh no.

I'll get it!
It's *you.*

Grandpa Winston!
What's the rumpus, my grandchildren?!
Honey, I didn't know your *dad* was coming...
Quite honestly, uh...his visit slippe my mind.

Slipped your mind? Benjamin! Tsk.
C'mere, Banira!

It's good to see you Winston!
How's my favorite daughter-in-law?

Hey, Pop.
Son...

Give your daddy a *hug!*
Oof! Stron

That's because I work **hard!**
Like steel!

"I work on my farm back at home!

Winston Bright and His Bright-Tones
"I work it out with the band!"

I just work!
Wow, Grandpa. You're amazing.
Oh, I've just got an appetite for ***living!***

That's why your dad and I made this plan for a little family reunion! After all, I haven't gotten to see much of you in the past few years.
SAFETY PRO

"Do you remember that summer you came to visit me?"
"Best. Summer. Ever."
"That was *so* fun."
"I remember, Dad--they came back all dirty and scraped-up!"

You've got to ***lighten up,*** Benjamin.
These kids aren't going to ***break*** if you let them out of your sight.
Well, technically, we ***could*** break--
Grandpa's talking to your daddy.
SAFETY

I bet you've still got them studying those ***Bright Family Safety Protocols,*** huh?
What? Er, um...

Well, I had a long trip here, and I'm ***hungry.***
Who wants Grandpa to buy dinner at that pizza place 'round the way?
Me!
Me!
Me!
Okay, Pop.

So you mean to tell me that for the past few weeks, y'all have been...what'd you call it, again?
Portal-hopping.
Portal-hopping, yeah. Sounds like some heavy science stuff.
The heaviest, Dad. You see, my theory was that the space-time continuum was like *folds* in fabric, so every point in space could actually be touched by *other* points in space and...
...and it was broken, and you and my grandchildren and my daughter-in-law had to travel from Planet A to Planet Z, fixin' it all up?
In simplest terms, yes, that's correct.
Mmm, I *love* the combination of pineapple and cashews on this.
You'll never catch *me* hoppin' no portals. But yes, this *is* good.

Grandpa, it's so much fun! You should try it.
Dad's *really* good at inventing stuff.

Oh, I'm okaaaaay...
You're *great* at it.

He even made our robot, Dusty!

Is that what you are? I thought Benjamin put some legs on the TV again.

Again?!

'our daddy as been an inventor since *day one.*
"Even when he was a baby, he was building all kinds of crazy gadgets.
"When he was ten, he built a hydroelectric car for him and the other kids to ride around in. A *car!*
"He was even in charge of repairing all the instruments in our family band!"

Your dad was a *wiz* on the melodica.
You never told us that!
You played in the band with Grandpa?

I'll tell you even more stories 'bout your dad while we spend the next few days taking a *culinary tour* of the city. Ramen for *everybody!*

Yay!
We've got a scheduling problem, Pop. Tomorrow morning we're going back to the resort planet.

Aw, mannnnnnnn...
Can't we just hang out with Grandpa for a few days?

Listen to your dad, kids. He's a busy man.

I want to hang out with Grandpa *and* party at the space water park.
Me too.

That's it! Of course! You kids are geniuses!

Grandpa could come *with* us!

I don't know-- Fleuben is only expecting us...
Don't be silly, Benjamin. There are enough free passes here for *all* of us.

Pleeeeease, Grandpa?
I bet they have some sort of campsite there. And you should *see* the buffet at this place.
They got ramen?
Space ramen!

I'll do it! Then I can say I've been to another planet--even if it is some cushy resort planet.

But what about this **portal** I suppose we'll be taking? What guarantee do I have that some bug won't fly in and crisscross my DNA?
Dad, please!

Is that a thing? Can it **do** that? Can I be a bug boy?
No, it's not a thing--DNA safety protocols were the **first** safeguards I installed.
Sheesh! Do you think I'm some kind of--I don't know--**mad scientist?**

It's 99 percent safe.
It's that 1 percent that worries me...

The next morning...
Okay, is everybody packed and ready to go?
All set!
This suit sure is *tight.*
You'll get used to it, Grandpa.
Where's your mom and Dusty?

They've gotta be around here somewhere...

Mom! Dusty! We're waiting for you.
Coming, honey!

Everybody ready?

Ready!

And do you *promise* that you'll try to forget about work while we're on vacation?
99 percent!

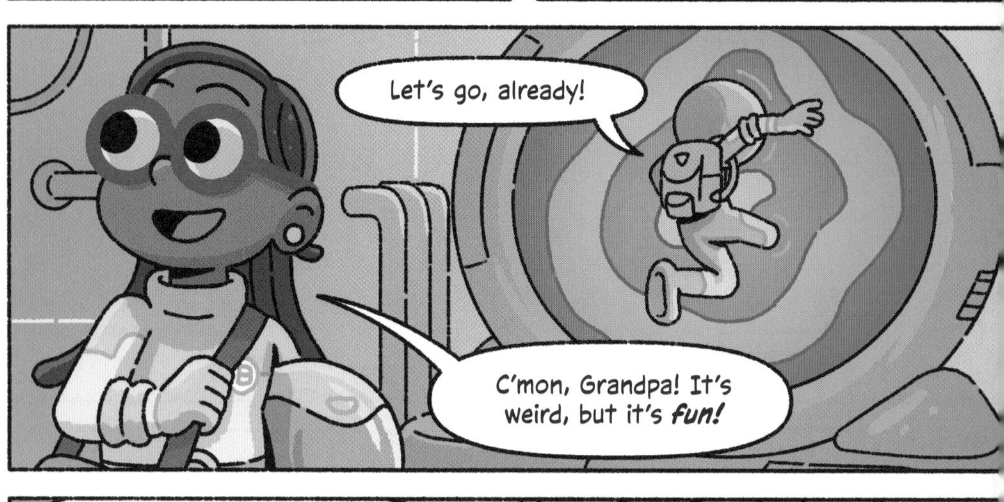
Let's go, already!
C'mon, Grandpa! It's weird, but it's *fun!*

It *can* be a bit disorienting, Pop, so please be careful...
Don't worry about me. As long as I've got my walking TV and don't turn into a bug, I'll be *fiiiiiiine...*

You kids weren't kidding--this *is* fun!
ley, kids!
Hi, Mom!
Hmm...
What's that *hmm* mean? Are you working?!
No, I'm getting some funny readings. It's probably nothing.
There's the other end of the portal! We're almost there!
I can practically *smell* the buffet!
POP
Wait. Something's not right.
Dad, look!

So, 99 percent, huh?
We should've gone out for ramen.

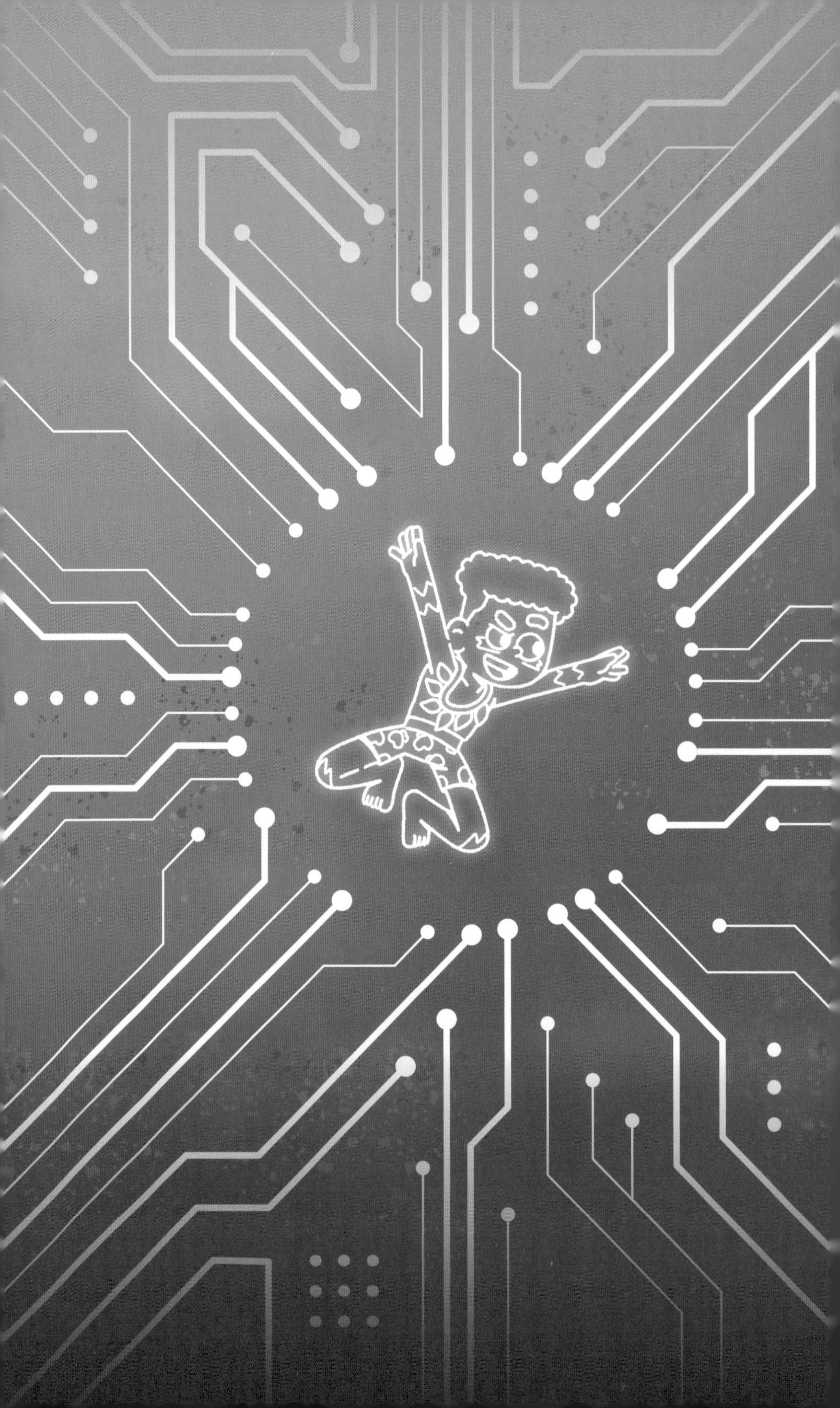

CHAPTER 2
IN SEARCH OF... SPACE RAMEN!

The explorer makes her way through the alien jungle, blissfully unaware that the foliage is teeming with life.
The noises of her new surroundings are strange--and alarming.
Huh?
CRACK
Just some native fauna, I guess.
But the explorer's bravery is stronger than her fear, and she continues on. And when she least expects it...
...the predator strikes!
Ahhh!

Gotcha, Nia!
Jayden!
What are you doing?!

I'm acclimating to our new home.

We've only been here a few ***hours.*** Put your clothes back on and follow me. Mom and Dad want you back at the campsite.

Aww. I liked being free from the shackles of clothing and ***civilization...***

Bright Family Vacation, Day 1.
Found him!
Great! Now the meeting can begin.
First, let's review the Bright Family Safety Protocols...
Groaannnn!
What? They're handy.

We *know* the protocols already, Dad.
And we *ignore* them all the time.

Okay, okay. Why don't you just give the situation report?
Yes! Thank goodness I brought my portable Smart Lecture Board.

As you can see, I've broken it down into three main elements, which I will break down even further...
Break it down, Dad!
Ahem. Yes. Thank you, Jayden.
Number one: The portal sent us to a mysterious *new* location, *not* the resort.
You hear that? We're not at the resort! That's science for you.
C'mon. I'm trying to be ***methodical*** about this.
Sorry, son. Carry on with the ***science!***

Number two: We appear to be in an undeveloped jungle biome. So far, no hostile flora or fauna.
But there's still hope, right? ***Right?!***

And three: The portal tech is offline, which means we cannot travel.
My conclusion: We should set up camp for tonight and tackle number three tomorrow. Questions?

Set up camp with what? We were supposed to be chilling in a fancy hotel!
I believe that I may be able to help with that...

...because I brought my *camping* backpack!
Dad, why did you bring your camping gear when we said we were going to a resort?

In case I didn't like my room.
I've got a tent! It'll be tight, but we'll make it work.
POP

I've got protein bars to keep us fed!
GRAMBAR
GRAMBAR

And I've got my trumpet for playing "Taps" at sunset. Because my philosophy is...

"Always think about what happens next!"

It's the Bright Scouts motto.

What are the *Bright Scouts?*
When your dad and his siblings were kids, I created our own family scout troop.
We had badges, a manual, camping trips--everything.
Including a motto.

I'm surprised you remember it.
It's only the basis of my entire scientific philosophy, Dad.

Oh. How about that?

And thinking about what happens next, I believe that we should--
Hold on a minute, son. *I* think what happens next is--
Um, who's the scientist with experience traveling to other worlds? Oh, that'd be me.
And who's the elder who knows best? This guy!

Well, *I* think what happens next is we explore a little bit more. Who's with me?
I'm with Mom.
I already covered the sectors of the jungle behind us. I say we go this way, toward the beach.

And you two, simmer down!
But he--
I was just--
Enough! We are stranded on an alien planet **together,** so you boys are going to have to learn how to get along.

Mom!
Dad!
Look!

Civilization! Well, the remains of one.
It's dusty, but it has good bones. I say we stay here tonight!
That's what I was going to say!
It looks like some sort of *abandoned exploration outpost.*
Yeah. But *why* was it abandoned, and b
who? Spoooooky.

Well, at least whoever lived here picked a planet with nice sunsets. Isn't this ***great?***

Maybe we should just retire for the evening.
We could all use some rest.
Just a minute there, son. Turn around.

Oh, wow.

Allow me to play a little somethin'. A view like that deserves a send-off.

Jazzy version of "Taps."
That was really nice, Dad.
Reminded me of being back home.
Yeah, that was great, Grandpa.
Aw, it's nothin'...
Night!
Night.
Night!
Night.
Night, everybody.
Sweet dream
TV with leg

Bright Family Vacation, Day 2.
You're up *already,* Grandpa?
Up you wake, Bright Family!
I've got coffee for the adults and protein bars for everyone!

Except you, my friend.
Unless Benjamin invented a way for you to *eat.*

Thanks for the coffee, Dad. Nice design.

I know a thing or two about survival, Mr. Big Scientist.
I *was* the leader of the Bright Scouts, after all.
But there were only *three* of us!

You and your brother and sister were the little toes, and I was the *big toe* on that foot!
That's only four toes--
You know what I mean!

Okay, okay--enough talk about toes. Let's have a family conversation about what we're going to actually *do* about our current situation.
I'm glad you brought that up, Banira, because last night I took the opportunity to write a *new* chapter of the Bright Family Safety Protocols!
I can read it to you all, if you'd like.
Bright Family Safety Protocols: So You're Stranded on a Mysterious Planet
Grooooaaaaannn!

What?
That's like *homework!* On *vacation!*

Safety has its place, son, but I have a better idea.
Go on...

KNOCK KNOCK
This place is **solid.**
With your help, we can make it a grade A shelter. Shouldn't take more than eight hours or so, I reckon...

Nope! That sounds like ***actual*** work! Just as bad as ***homework!***

I have another idea: Why don't we just do...nothing? At least for now?

Nothing?
At all?

Think about it--we've got supplies and shelter.

The weather on this planet is wonderfully mild.
78°F 20%
According to Dusty's sensors, it's 78 degrees, with 20 percent humidity.

The local fauna doesn't seem that interested in eating us.
Can I keep all of them?

And the geography looks pleasant!
I think we should spend some time at that beach.

It sounds a little...dangerous.
And slightly... frivolous.

Dangerous!
Frivolous!
Dangerous!
Frivolous!

Hey, where'd they go?

Look, a note.

Gone to the beach with the kids!
You two have fun together!
Love, B.♡

ave fun? They
eft their wrist
ommunicators
behind!
That's *definitely* a violation of the safety protocols!
And this when we could be securing camp...

I'll be in my makeshift lab, working on the portal problem, Mr. Big Toe. Follow me, Dusty!
I'm going to do some shelter improvements. C'mon, TV!

Dusty?

TV? Er, Dusty?

eanwhile...
Woo-hoo!
Hahahaha!
Hey, kids! It's probably time to go back now.
Okay, Mom!

Mom, are Dad and Grandpa mad at each other?
What? No! They love each other--a lot.

But they're always kind of...arguing. Is it because they're so *different?*
Different? Ha! Those Bright men are *exactly* the same.
They just express their Bright-ness in their own way.

All they need is time to figure that out. Anyway, let's get back for dinner.
I wonder what your grandpa is cooking up. Probably not space ramen, I'm sorry to say.

Who needs space ramen when you've got all this tasty fruit? I'm actually okay with not making it to the resort.
About the resort... kids, I have a confession to make.
Hold on. Something's not right...

CRACK
CHOMP!
Shh!

There's something following us...
GULP
Y' evuh get th' feelin'...

...that you're being *watched?*
It's you!

Back at camp.
TOK TOK TOK
I fixed up the exterior while you were in here portal gazing. So how's that going, Mr. Safety Protocols?
Slowly but surely, Dad. That's how you win the science race.
You should've been out there working with me! At least you woul have gotten something *done.*
This is work, too! I'm only trying to fix the portal to get us *home.* Nothing *important* or anything...

I didn't say it wasn't important!
But you implied it!
I didn't mean it that way!
It sure sounded like you did!

Well, I'm sorry! Happy?
Yes! Thank you! Apology accepted!
Fine. Time to start working on dinner.
Where *are* Banira and th kids, anyway? They shou have been back by now.

Banira!
Nia! Jayden!

Bright Scouts search party?
You read my mind.

Wait, ***did*** you read my mind?
What? No! That's ridiculous.

Or ***is it?***

Haha! You should have seen the look on your face.
C'mon, Dad. Mind-reading machines don't exist.
Only because you haven't invented one yet! I know you...

It's getting dark. Let's get search partying...
Kids! Honey!
Hello?

Anything?
Nope.

Dad, I'm getting worried.
Son.

I know that you and I don't see eye to eye all the time, but I won't rest--*we* won't rest--until we find our family.
Yes, sir!

SNIFF
SNIFF
It can't be!
Can't be what?

That aroma! It's...

It's...
It's *what?!*

I don't know about you, but I could swear I smell *space ramen.*
But Dad...

...that's *impossible!*

CHAPTER 3
THE LAST RESORT

e last left the Bright Family stuck on an uncharted 'anet--or were they? Banira and the kids ran into a familiar presence in the jungle--or did they?
And Benjamin and Grandpa Winston smelled space ramen--but how? These questions and more will be answered in the conclusion of the Bright Family Vacation Saga...
...or will they?*
It's you!
I could swear I smell space ramen.
*They will.
Dad, this isn't the time to be thinking about food.
But it's there, in the air!
Can a plant mimic the complex melding of spices in space ramen broth?
Nature is a wonder, Dad. And when you multiply it by thousands of planets...the mathematics of its possible beauty boggles the mind.

That was pretty poetic, Benjamin. You should write that down.
Thanks, Dad.

But the galaxy's potential for beauty and wonder means it also has potential for ***everything else,*** too.

"Somewhere in this jungle, there might be ***carnivorous alien plants*** looking for their next meal.

"Or Jayden might have made friends with ***cute aquatic creatures*** and become the ruler of their undersea kingdom."
"That seems unlikely."
"Have you ***met*** your grandson?"
"Fair point."

"And then there are ***extraterrestrial dinosaurs.*** We can't rule ***anything*** out!"

BONK
?!
BIG SIPP

Big Sipper? What in the world...
BIG SIPP

BIG IPPE
Hmm.

CRUNCH
What was that?!
Boy, if there's an extraterrestrial dinosaur...
That was just a ***hypothesis.*** I don't seriously think there's a--

Giant robot!
You forgot to mention those!
I didn't think of them! Run, Dad!
Take. Out. The. Trash.
I hope Banira and the kids didn't get trampled by this robot!
Banira Suzuki-Bright is a *boss!* She can handle *anything!*
Yes! That's true! Banira rules!
As a science hero *and* a mom!

You married very well!
That's also true! I did! I'm very fortunate! Why are we yelling?!
Because we're being chased by a giant robot!

Down there!

But you're right--we have to trust that Banira and the kids know what they're doing.

And we also have to take care of ourselves while we search, so that means...

...time to *hydrate!*

GLUG
GLUG
GLUG
GLUG

I'm glad to see that you remembered your canteen.
Hey, once a Bright Scout, *always* a Bright Scout.
Speaking of hydration...

...this **Big Sipper** obviously indicates that an intelligent species is somewhere nearby--and that it likes iced tea.

Ooh, iced tea sounds *good.* This little fella wouldn't happen to have a soda fountain inside, would he?
Dad, I made Dusty to be a sophisticated autonomous robotic helper, not a drink dispenser.

Hey, it's a good idea for the *next* model.
No, Dad.

Okay--I think we've lost it. Let's get back to searching for Banira and the kids.

Vhile we're at it, maybe I can gure out what's going on with this wrist communicator.
If I can get it to work, I can track their location!
TAP TAP

Or we could track them the Bright Scouts way...

Jayden's footprints!
And Banira's and Nia's--they must have come this way!

Dad... behind you...

Uh-oh...

Dad, follow Dusty! Dusty, follow the tracks!
Following!
Take. Out. The. Trash.
Why does it keep saying that?
I don't know. But let's not stop and ask it!
Keep up, young man!

Huff! Huff! Huff!
How do you move so fast?!

How? I exercise, son!

Oof!

The tracks stop here!
There's an elevator!

Going up?
Yes!
PSSHT!
Push!
No room! Take the next one, robot!
FWUMP
We did it!
Bright Scouts for the win!

It's nice that they have elevator music in space.
This song is huff! so familiar. It's...something Brazilian, right?
Good ear, boy. That's "Mas Que Nada," if I'm not mistaken.

Get ready, Dad.
PSSHHT
I'm with you, son.

Ahhhhhhhh!

Jayden?!
Dad! Grandpa! Dusty!

Where's your mom? And Nia? Are they okay?
Okay? Are you kidding?

We're great!
You made it!
Hi, everyone!
I'm happy to see you, but...there's a giant robot after us!
Do you mean this giant robot, Mr. Bright?
Fleuben?!
This LitterBot was simply trying to pick up some trash that blew over the wall!
Ohhhh.
But Fleuben--where'd you come from?
What's going on?!
Well, it's kind of a funny story...

"...that began when the kids and I were walking through the jungle."
Yes, it's *me,* Bright Family...

...Fleuben, your favorite intergalactic resort manager!

But what are you doing *here,* on this uncharted planet?
Uncharted? Are you kidding? Thi is *my* planet!

Your planet?! But where are the luxury accommodations?
Where's the space ramen, man?
Didn't your mom let you in on her plan?

Her plan?
Say *what*
I can explain.

Follow me. It's right through here...
SIGH
We demand answers!
Here we are!
Uh-huh.
A wall. Incredible.
It *is* incredible, Bright Family, for ingeniously hidden in this wall is...
...my fancy freight elevator!
Right this way. Resort level, please, elevator!
We're waiting, Mom.
Don't think this fancy elevator made us forget that you owe us an explanation.

So...when your grandpa and dad started butting heads back on Earth, I thought it'd be a great idea to get them talking.
Like, ***really*** talking.
"I made a call to Fleuben and told him my idea. Luckily, he had something ***perfect*** in mind.
"And right before we made our portal jump, I had Dusty change our coordinates to the ones Fleuben gave me.
"We also 'fixed' the portal so we couldn't just go back when your dad figured out we hadn't hit our target."
"Mom, that's so...crafty! Nice one!"
"I learned from the best, Jayden."

But...where are we ***now?***
You're ***almost*** exactly where you intended to be--the portal simply took you to the other side of the resort.

The ***other*** side?!

Yes! The jungle is a more...rustic area where guests can rough it if they like. But this is the real resort! Welcome!
Space ramen! Yummmmmm!
Antigravity beds! I bet the science behind this is amazing.
TRY OUR SUPER KING SIZED ANTIGRAVITY BEDS
But what about Dad? And Grandpa Winston?
Yeah. Shouldn't we get them, too?
We could do that, but...well, I have something else to show you. Follow me.

RESORT EMPLOYEES ONLY
It's right in here...
Welcome to our observation room, where we can keep track of everything going on in the other part of the resort.
It's Dad and Grandpa!
And Dusty!
They seem like they're getting along.
They are definitely ***bonding,*** as people say.

They *are* safe down there, right?
Of course!
They're not in any *real* danger. Right now, they're basically *camping.*
And we can watch hem figure out how o get to the resort from the comfort of this theater?
Precisely!
In that case...
Bring on the space kettle corn, Fleuben! That's a thing, right?
It certainly is. And I must say that *our* space kettle corn is the best in the galaxy.

And that's what happened. I'm sorry, honey. I just wanted you and your dad to have some quality time.
We're at Fleuben's resort?! And you an the kids were watchi us the *whole time*
You were only down there for... ***five hours,*** Benjamin.
Are you sur It certain ***felt*** longer
And hoo boy--I am ***starving.*** They got anything to eat around here?
Grandpa, you have ***no*** idea.
GRRUMBLE

And that's when the Bright Family's vacation really began. There was feasting!

Relaxing!

And family time!

But all vacations must come to an end.
Thanks again, Fleuben. We'd love to stay, but the kids have school tomorrow.
There'll always be a warm bowl of space ramen waiting for you at this resort, Bright Family!
With extra...

...spiiiiiiiiiice?

Woo-hoo! Home again, home again, jiggly pig!
I don't think that's how that goes.
Who cares?!

Sooooo... anybody up for some late-night jazz? There's a jam session at a club downtown.
WEEKLY JAZZ JAM DOWNTOWN
Not me! I'm gonna find out if antigravity beds can actually work here on Earth.
And I'm beat from all that relaxing.

I'm going to read the latest issue of ***Science Hero Weekly.*** You boys have fun together.

What are you looking for, Dad?
I've been carrying this in my pack for ***years.*** Figure it's time to finally give it to you. After all...

...you've earned it.
BRIGHT SCOUTS • MASTER SCOUT

Aw, Dad...

Thank you.

So...
You want me to bring my horn?
How *else* will you join the jam session?
Let's do it, then!
Now let's talk about my idea for a robot that's also a soda dispenser...
I'm serious. It's genius!
Let's just focus on the jazz, okay?
Whatever you say, Dad. Whatever you say.

CHAPTER 4
GATHERING OF THE GALAXIES

CAT → CHAT
DOG → CHIEN
COW → VACHE
I have your progress reports for the semester, students. Here you go, Mr. Bright.

I know you can do better.
Hmph.

RIIIING!!!

RIIIING!!
Remember, class: These need to be signed by ***Monday!***

Nia! Hey, Nia! Wait up!
Hey, Jayden.
What's wrong?
Did you get your progress report?
Yeah.
Ohhhhhh yeah. Sure did. You?
How was yours?
Ugh...

Hmm.
This is...

...almost as bad as mine!
It's not funny! This has ***never*** happened to me before.

Well, there's a first time for everything. You should see ***my*** report.

Pee-***yew!***

Ha. I can smell it from here.
Right?!

But seriously, Jayden--I don't know what *happened.*
Maybe you've got *cross-dimensional brain fog.*

What?
Or the *portal flu!*
There's no such thing as the *portal flu.* You're making that up.
Are you sure? You *do* feel kinda warm.

Cut it out--I'm not sick! But...you might be onto something.
I might?

Haven't you felt a little... *different* since we've been through all those portals?
There's so much *out there,* out there!
Everything at home seems so small when you compare it to the whole multiverse.
It makes you wonder-- what's the point of school, or progress reports, or *anything,* really?
Outside the Bright Family home.
I *do* miss the space ramen.
I miss it, too, Jayden. ⁝Sigh⁝

Hey, Dusty.
Where's Dad?
In his lab?
Okay. Thanks,
buddy.
HELLO!

Yo, Dad.
We've, uh,
got **progress reports!**
Great! Let's talk
about them when
your mom gets
home.

I just need
to finish up with
something here...

He's doing stuff with his terraforming goggles, but he said we'll talk when Mom gets home.
Okay, we've got some time. Maybe we should come up with a strategy for how to break it to them?
You start cutting the onions, and I'll work on our stories--
Hellooooooo, Bright Family! You ll know what day it --progress report day! Let's check em out and get to celebrating!

A little while later...
So let me get this straight--both of you bombed?
Bombed is a bit of an overstatement, Mom.
Ka-boom!

But what happened? I mean, Jayden I can see. But you, Nia...

Hey!

I'm sorry--that was unfair. But your father and I expect much more from you kids.

These progress reports are way below your abilities. There have to be consequences.
So as of right now, all your weekend activities are canceled.

But I was supposed to go to Natalie and Caroline's birthday party!
And I was gonna read **comics** all weekend!

Nope, and nope. Instead, you two are coming with **me** this weekend.
To your boring **conference?!** Nooooo!
Mom! Please! Be reasonable!

This **is** me being reasonable. This weekend, you two are going to be my interns. Maybe a bit of **work** will straighten you out.

Work?! Aw, Mom!
Are we at least going to take a portal to the conference?
No way. Portal travel is making you kids soft. We're doing this the old-fashioned way...

...by traveling in my supersonic, transcontinental ***jump jet.***
This thir is, like, a ***antique,*** M
It's not an antique, Jayden. It's a ***classic!*** And it's served me well since I started out as a science explorer.
Everybody buckled in back there? Okay-- here we go! Three... two...one...
BLAST OFF!

Wahhhh!
Aaahhh!
!!!

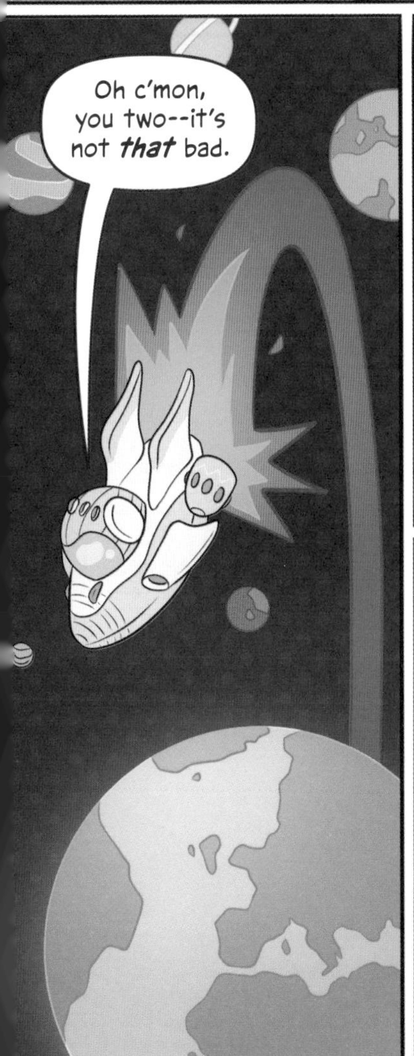
Oh c'mon, you two--it's not *that* bad.

Okay, reaching cruising altitude now.
So how long will this trip take?

About an hour or so.
An *hour?!*

No complaining on my jet. Think some deep thoughts! Enjoy the ride!
Why didn't Dad have to come and work, too?
Because he's got important research to do.
Research?! He's just playing with his terraforming program.
Yeah--he's playing games! Why does he get to play games?!
Hold on--I'm getting a distress signal from a whale rescue ship. And it's nearby!
Dusty, circle the jet and be ready to pick me up!
WHOOSH!

Anyway, Dad didn't have to come because ***Dad*** isn't the one who brought home such disappointing grades.
ECOEXPLORER

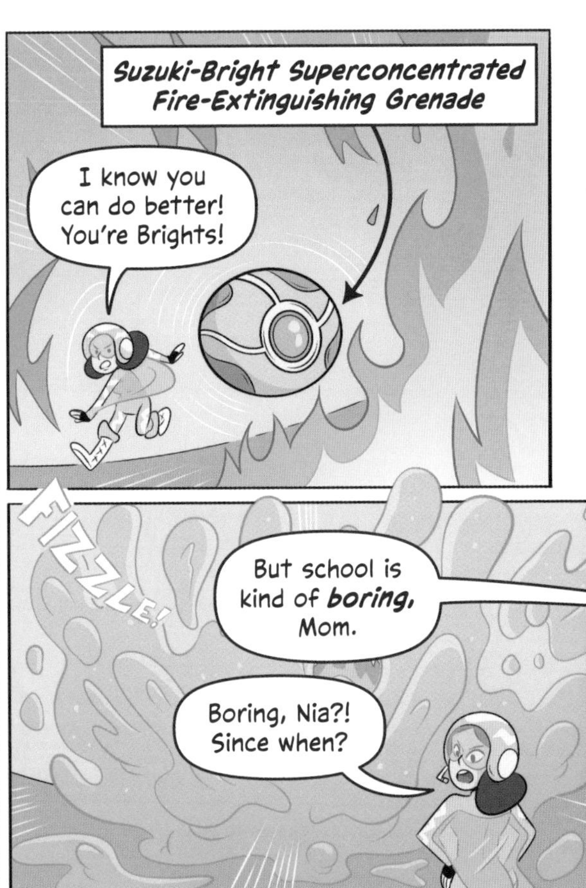

Suzuki-Bright Superconcentrated Fire-Extinguishing Grenade
I know you can do better! You're Brights!
FIZZLE!
But school is kind of ***boring,*** Mom.
Boring, Nia?! Since when?

It's not portal-hopping, that's for sure.
Portal travel and school are ***entirely*** different things, Jayden.
ECO EX

Let's talk more about this later. We're approaching our destination.
Where are we going, anyway?
Didn't I tell you? Only one of the neatest places in the world...

...Neosaka!
Neosaka? The artificial island city off the coast of Japan?
Precisely. You know, your father worked on a lot of the critical terraforming infrastructure for this place.

Nice landing!
Thanks, Nia.
SMOOTH GLIDE!

What happened to *Osaka* Osaka?
It's still right next door. They just built this one because there was a big demand for it. They needed *more* Osaka, so...voilà!
Did they consider calling it...*Mo'Saka?*

I can't wait to explore. The geoengineering of artificial islands is *super* interesting.
While you do that, I'm going to try *all* the okonomiyaki* stands.
*Japanese cabbage pancakes--a popular street food now and in the future!

Remember, kids-- this is a *work* trip.
Awww.

Wow! Look at this place! Does it have a swimming pool?
Probably, but you two are going to be too busy to swim.

I'll have your bags taken to your rooms. Enjoy the ***boring science conference,*** Dr. Suzuki-Bright.
I will! I'm sure it's going to be ***very*** dull.
???

What's going on, Mom? What kind of conference is this, anyway?
Shh! Not here. The ***boring conference*** is just an elaborate cover story.

This way, kids. Then I'll tell you what's *actually* going on.
"I got the idea while we were at Fleuben's resort. There we were, Earthlings, peacefully interacting with a vast variety of interstellar beings.
"I had a vision of a future where the people of the galaxy shared ideas, knowledge, and culture!
"But it had to start somewhere.
"It took months of intergalactic conference calls and logistics emails, but all that effort finally paid off!"
Fleuben, can you mute your microphone? I'm getting a lot of echo.
Oops! Sorry.

We organized the inaugural Transdimensional and Intergalactic Science and Goodwill Summit!

We're having it in Neosaka because I want the delegates to see what Earth can bring to the cosmic table, but we don't want to reveal that aliens exist...yet. Hence all the secrecy.
Awesome, Mom! And sneaky.
Mom, this is *amazing!*

So what do you need us to do? Mediate a scientific discussion? Deliver a lecture on our experiences?
Are we audiovisual support?
No, but your job is still *incredibly* important...

"You'll be handing out souvenir tote bags and helping out however you're asked."
Welcome to the first Transdimensional and Intergalactic Science and Goodwill Summit.
Have fun having fun. Enjoy your tote bag.

I can't believe it. We're in the coolest town on Earth, and we're stuck at the swag table.
The most important scientific conference in the galaxy is happening meters away, and we're handing out tote bags.
Tote bags!
There isn't even any free local candy in here. Being an intern is the worst.

Here come some people.
One tote bag, coming up.

Here's your complimentary tote bag, ma'am. You can, uh, carry your son in it?
Um...

nd look at this cute little fella! What's ur name, little guy?
I am Prime Minister Anfonio Braxas, intern! And this is my daughter, Fielgorf!

But...she's so...big. And you're so...little. How...

Ahem! That's how the life cycle of our species works--our children begin life as titanic, clumsy babies, then slowly but steadily shrink into compact and nimble adults like me. Interns should know these things!
A reverse life cycle... fascinating.
The galaxy is ***wild...***

Look at the time! I'm late for a lecture. Interns!
I assume your duties include entertaining the children of conference delegates? Very well.

I'll see you later, Fielgorf!
Mom ***did*** say to help out however we're asked.
She sure did!
Hi, Fielgorf. I'm Nia Bright, and this is my brother, Jayden. We're from Earth!
Nice to meet yo both!

So...I say we ditch the tote bag stand. Who's with me?
Me!
Me!

Cover for us, Dusty! C'mon, Fielgorf.

Can we explore e city? I've read about Neosakan onomiyaki, and I ally want to try some.
You're speaking my language, Fielgorf. You ever been to Fleuben's resort? Their space ramen is...
SMOOCH!

It's Mom! Hide!

Phew! That was close.
I don't understand. You wish to *avoid* your mother?
Technically, we shouldn't be taking you out of the hotel, aliens being *top secret* and all.
So if we're going to hit the town, you'll need a disguise.
Ah--subterfuge! I love it!
Psst! Are you all getting out of here?
We *might* be planning on taking a tour, culinary and otherwise, of Neosaka. Want to come?
Affirmative!
I'm Gilbort.
Oh! I didn't know you had a *Braxsonian* with you.
A *Pelosian*?

What's
appening here?
I'm confused.
Our worlds have been rivals for hundreds of cycles!
The Braxsonians know what they did.
The Pelosians started it!

My father says--
Nope!

This conference is supposed to be
bout pandimensional and galactic
nderstanding--not
ld rivalries between our parents.

You get me?

We get you, Nia Bright.
When you put it like that... truce!

Great! Now let's check out Neosaka... together!
Okonomiyaki!

Later, back at the conference...
Excellent keynote speech, Dr. Suzuki-Bright! This conference is going to be *great!*
CLAP
CLA
I hope so. There's a lot that could go wrong with these different cultures interacting, but also *so much* that could go *right.*

Er--speaking of *so much that could go wrong...*
I left Fielgorf here, with those two interns! It's a Pelosian plot--a plot, I say!
And Gilbort was last seen in the company of *your* child! So *you're* the plotter!

Whoa--what's going *on* here?
Well, the Braxsonians have been at odds with the Pelosians for *forever,* and vice versa. It's a classic *planet versus moon* rivalry.
If my Fielgorf isn't found immediately, this means war!
I was going to say that! You copied me--again!
Sigh.

CHAPTER 5
THE WATERMELONS OF WRATH

CLASH OF THE SUPER KAIJU!
I declare *Clash of the Super Kaiju!*... a total ***masterpiece!*** Best film ever made!
The battle between Supersaur and Supersimian was ***epic.*** I can't believe they ended up joining forces!
It was like watching the titanic creatures of our Braxsonian myths come to ***life!***
That's funny--I was thinking they were like Pelosian myths!

We have myths, but we don't have popcorn! So I get the last handful!
But I wanted the last kernels. Give me that sweet popcorn with the salty seaweed bits, Braxsonian!
It's mine, Pelosian!
Hey! How about you get back to talking about your shared mythology.
And calling each other by your first names!
There's enough for everybody, okay?
You're right, Nia. Sorry, Gilbort.
Apologies, Fielgorf.
All this arguing is attracting too much attention.
We need better disguises for you before we eat.
Everybody...

KAIJUBILEE
...I think I found a solution.

Moments later.
Gotta hand it to you, Jayden. This is cool.
Isn't it?!

Rawr!
I love it!

We blend right in!

And bonus: We. Look. *Great.*

I think the restaurant is right down here...

Pretty sure I could spend the rest of my *life* in this alley.
Ah! Here we are!

W!
MIYAKI
Four okonomiyaki for me and my friends, please!
Do you think our parents are wondering where we are?
I bet they haven't even noticed we're *gone.*

Meanwhile...
...Braxonian treachery!
?

...Pelosian skulduggery!
!

Excuse me, but is everything okay in there?
Everything is fine! It's just a, uh, private viewing of a sports contest!
The Braxsonians versus the Pelosians... doing sports! Against each other!

What's happening in there, robot?

Dusty! Whatever you do...

...*don't* let anybody in!
Enough talk! Time for *action!*
I couldn't agree with you *more!*

Please! Let's all just **calm down** and get back to the conference.
Calm down? **Calm down?!** This is not a time for calming down--it's a time for...**uncalming up!**

Uncalming up?

Exactly.

I accuse the Braxsonians of spiriting my child away in a brazen attempt to...
...I don't know what! But I accuse them!

Just like a Pelosian to accuse another of what they are guilty of.
You have spirited *my* child away in a brazen attempt to...you know what you did!

Do not!
Do too!
Let's just say that *neither* of you knows what happened, and start from there.

I'm certain we can clear up this misunderstanding if we take a step back and methodically analyze its origins!

This isn't the time for methodical analysis! You and your children are part of this plot against us!
Yes! Exactly!

Why would we do that? I organized this conference to be a beacon of unity, and my children are committed to the cause as well!

No, they're in league with ***you*** and plotting against ***us!***
They're in league with ***you,*** and plotting against ***us!***

Lunch has arrived, Dr. Suzuki-Bright. Maybe a meal will calm them down?
Good thinking. We'll discuss intergalactic conflict resolution over lunch.
Maybe some food will make them less cranky.

PLUCK!

For **Fielgorf!** For **Braxas!**
Oof!

Of course you know that this... means...***war!***

Negative. Food does not make them less cranky.

Pelosians... to arms!

Onward, Braxsonians!

This is *not* happening. A *food fight* is *not* breaking out at my conference to promote intergalactic understanding and peaceful cooperation.

I'd say it's more of a *culinary skirmish.*
Not helpful!

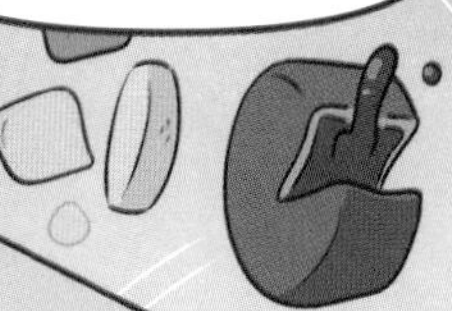
I'm calling Nia and Jayden. If they're with Fielgorf and Gilbort, they need to get back here before this *culinary skirmish* becomes an all-out **FOOD WAR**.
Does this mean I should push the "Time Travel: Multiple Alternate Futures" seminar back?
RING RING
It's time travel, so I guess *when* it happens isn't so important...

Meanwhile, at Wow! Okonomiyaki...
I rate that okonomiyaki five stars. What do you two think?
I've never had cabbage or pancakes before, but they are an excellent fusion.
The sauce! The mayonnaise! The moving bonito flakes!
Whoever invented this delicacy deserves all the accolades.
So what should we do now? Go to an arcade? Get seconds?
Why not both?
Great idea, Gilbort! More okonomiyaki, and then the arcade!

Uh-oh.
What's up?
RING RING

Mom's calling.
You think she realized we're not handing out tote bags?
BLEEP

Uh, hi, Mom. What's up?
Nia! Thank goodness. Where ***are*** you?!

Well, Jayden and I met these two cool alien kids, and we thought we should show them around--
Well, those ***cool alien kids*** are the children of Prime Minister Braxas and Empress Nacreeb. You need to get them back to the hotel ***now!*** Or else...

"...it's ***war!***"
We're on our way! Let's go, everybody!
I'll be back!

Shouldn't we *do* something?
You're right. We should. That's why I called the kids.

The kids?!
If we interfere, we'll fix a symptom and stop a food ***fight.***
With the kids' help, maybe we can cure the disease and prevent a food ***war.***

Dusty! Any sign of them?

Hi, Mom! We brought you some okonomiyaki.
Thank you, Jayden, but I'm *really* not hungry. What are you kids *wearing?!*
Actually, never mind.
I'm sorry we were gone for so long, Mom. We were just having such a good time hanging out with Gilbort and Fielgorf.
You made a mistake.
But maybe that kind of *hangout* is exactly what our current situation needs.
Gilbort and Fielgorf, I presume?
Yes, ma'am.
Your parents are worried sick about you, and because of the grudge between Braxsonians and Pelosians, a war is breaking out.
I need you to show them that peace is possible!
We'll work together!
And lead by example!

Aaahhh!
Giant monsters of legend!
Flee!

Braxas, this is a threat neither of us can defeat alone.
Are you proposing what I believe you're proposing?
Yes...

...the first-ever Braxsonian-Pelosian ***alliance!***
Together, we shall overcome. To arms!

Hey! **Hey!** Dad, it's **me!**

Stop--

Arrrggghh!

This is... not going well.
What are you talking about? This is ***awesome!***
We have to do something. Jayden, follow me.

There's more of them!
Hey! Please! Hold on for just a moment.
Renew the assault--with salt!

They won't listen!
They don't recognize you. Take off your hoods!
Oh!
Why didn't we think of that?

Hold your fire! It's us--Fielgorf and Gilbort!

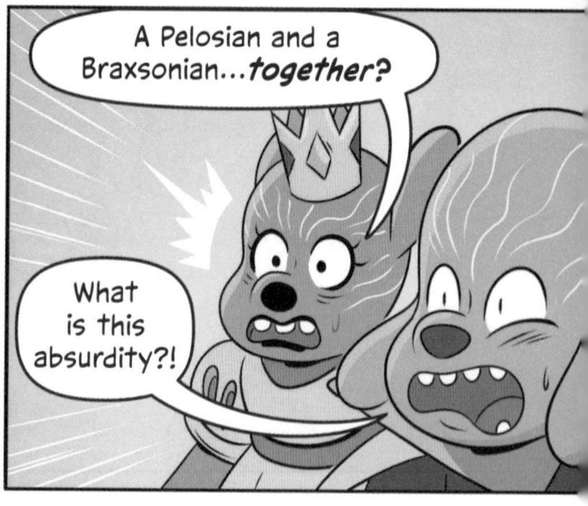
A Pelosian and a Braxsonian...***together?***
What is this absurdity?!

They're working together, just like ***you,*** Prime Minister Braxas and Empress Nacreeb.

At first, they weren't happy about hanging out together.
But they learned that it's a lot easier to get along than it is to hold a grudge.

We're sorry about leaving the conference. Jayden and I didn't mean to start a diplomatic incident. We just wanted to explore a new place with new friends.
It's too bad kids from different galaxies don't get to come together like this more often.
Indeed.
Absolutely.

I'm just glad you're back, Gilbort.
Likewise, Fielgorf.

Glad that's settled. But who's going to clean up this mess?
I elect my diplomat daughter and her little brother because before they fixed everything, they helped break it.
I guess that's fair.
Aw!

The next day...
What a successful conference, Dr. Suzuki-Bright! Speaking on behalf of all Braxsonians, we look forward to the next one.
And thank *you,* Nia and Jayden. You brought our children together and showed us the folly of our old ways!
All credit goes to the kaiju costumes.
Jayden!
It was so cool hanging out with you two.
Totally!
Thanks to you, we're going to be pen pals!
Bye, everybody!

RRRRUMBLE!

All right, kids. Locked in a course for home and letting the autopilot take over.
After we put on our space suits, anybody up for an in-flight movie?

Kids?

Is everything okay?
Yeah...no...I don't know.

Is this about your progress report? I think I overreacted. I'm sorry for making you feel bad about that.

Thanks, Mom.

I guess I'm just...a little sad. This weekend was *so* cool. Meeting those kids, helping broker peace between old rivals...and now what?

It's just that...after all the *stuff* we've seen across the galaxy, school back on Earth just seems...
...kinda *boring!*
Yep! That's it.

I still *like* school, and I love to learn, but I can't stop thinking about how much *more* is out there.

C'mere, you two!
SQUEEZE!
Oof!

Dusty, please take care of the landing. Kids, I have an idea, and I need to call your dad.

Later that evening...
What do you think they're working on down there?
I don't know, but Mom was really excited about it.
Nia! Jayden! Come down to the lab. We have something to show you!

What's going on?
You'll see. Ready, Benjamin?
Just putting on the finishing touches. Okay... done!

You two gave me a lot to think about this weekend, and I realized that your father's current terraforming work might be a solution to our problem. Benjamin?
You see, my project isn't a ***game***--it's a ***reality.*** I've been using nanotech, portals, and robots to experiment with terraforming an out-of-the-way planetoid.
But your mom had a brilliant idea for a practical application of the tech, so we cooked up a little proof of concept to show you.

So you're terraforming a ***planetoid?*** Cool! But what does that have to do with us?
Please say kaiju planet, please say kaiju planet...
You two have ***everything*** to do with it. You ***inspired*** it.
Show them, Benjamin.

We're going to start an intergalactic *middle school.*
Pretty cool. But Planet Kaiju would have been *way* cooler.

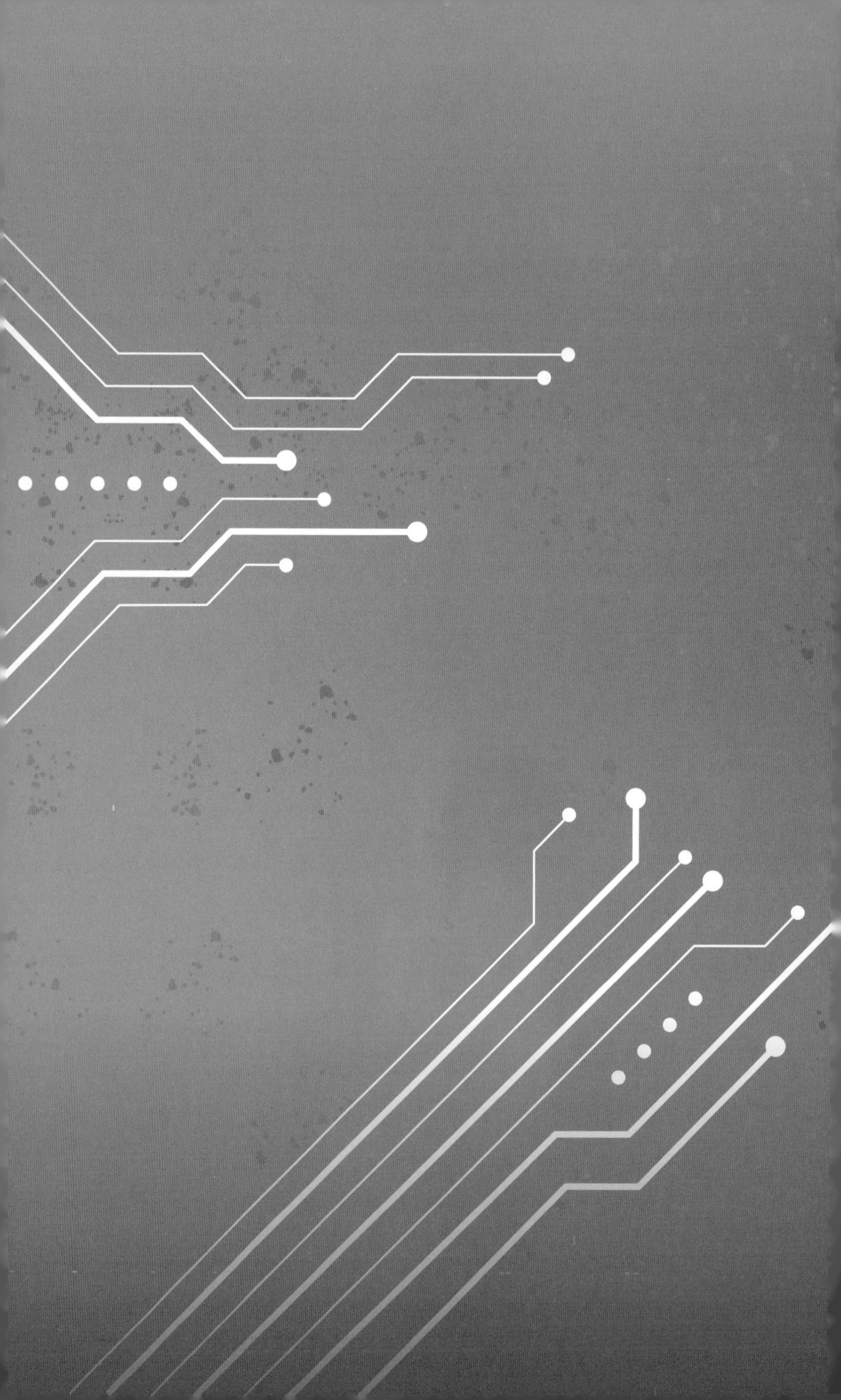

ABOUT THE AUTHOR

GABE SORIA is the creator of the Midnight Arcade series (Penguin Workshop) and the cocreator of the comic book *MegaGhost*. His other works include DC Comics' *Batman '66*, *Fakespeare in the Park*, a tie-in novel for Cartoon Network's *Regular Show* (Penguin Workshop), and the best-selling Audible Original *Foreverywhere*, created with Steve Burns of *Blue's Clues* and Steven Drozd of the band The Flaming Lips. He lives in New Orleans, where he's currently writing an original fantasy adventure trilogy for Penguin Workshop.

ABOUT THE ILLUSTRATORS

RAFA RIBS is a Brazilian artist currently living in São Paulo. He has worked as a character designer and visual development artist for animation and games for the last six years. He loves drawing imaginary universes and filling them with otherworldly characters and stories. Besides drawing, he likes playing indie games and going to music festivals.

VINCENT BATIGNOLE started his professional journey working on Serena Valentino and Ted Naifeh's comic series GloomCookie. Now living in Paris, he illustrates and writes for various international clients while earning a master's degree in cinema history and film analysis. When he's not drawing, you can find him playing video games, watching scary movies, or rummaging through book stores to grow his gigantic collection of manga drawn by CLAMP.

ABOUT THE COLORIST

WARREN WUCINICH is a comic book creator and part-time carny who has been lucky enough to work on such cool projects as *Invader ZIM*, *Courtney Crumrin*, and *Cat Ninja*. He is also the cocreator of the YA graphic novel *Kriss: The Gift of Wrath*. He currently resides in Boston, Massachusetts, where he spends his time making comics, rewatching '80s television shows, and eating all the tacos.

ONE BIRTHDAY
IN TIME

WRITTEN BY
GABE SORIA
ILLUSTRATED BY
SEAN DOVE
COLORS BY
SAM BENNETT

Today's breakthrough was incredible! But I should be heading home.
Got anything special planned for the evening, Dr. Bright?

No? Not that I can recall, at least.

ZZZT!

Whoa! What was *that?*
Huh. It almost felt like time-traveling tachyons... anyway, good night!

THE SWEET SCIENCE
I feel like I'm forgetting something...

HAPPY BIRTHDAY
Dad!
Hi, honey!

Did you get my cake?
Happy birthday, buddy!
Uh, Banira-- can I talk to you for a second? In the other room?

I'm not mad... but you forgot Jayden's cake, didn't you?
I made an important breakthrough at work today...and it slipped my mind.
But it's no excuse.

Well, the bakery's closed now. There's a box of NanoBake mix in the kitchen, but the side effects...

That's it! The bakery is closed *now,* but it wasn't closed an hour ago.
Yes, dear. That's how time works--open then, closed now.

Not necessarily. What if I could remind myself...back then?
You mean... time travel?
Ha! No, time travel is completely *improbable.* But...

What are *those?*
They're prototypes for a tachyon-powered memory aid.

I think I can use it to "nudge" my past brain to remember Jayden's cake.
KNOCK! KNOCK!
So...like a quantum physics alarm clock that you can set *after* you were supposed to wake up?
Exactly.
Mom! Daaaaaad! The birthday boy wants cake!
The not-birthday girl wants cake, too!
Patience! We're... figuring it out!

The kids are getting restless, and when they get restless...things happen.
I know. But if my theory is correct, this should take almost no time at all.

GROAN
Sending tachyon particles to remind myself to pick up the cake in three...
...two...
...one...

My hope is that we can ride the time stream and arrive at the right moment to remind my past self to grab Jayden's cake.
Hmm. Sounds iffy.

It's not like it's ***highly experimental science*** that plays around with ***memories.*** Oh wait...

Anyway, if my calculations are correct, we should be arriving at the right spot in time...now!

Hey--it's our first date! We were so cute back then...
Whoops! Rode the time stream too far. Let's back up--or, er, go forward.

Benjamin, look--it's the day the adoption became final!
That was one of the happiest days of our lives!

Oh! Remember our trip to the zoo?
How could I forget Jayden ***diving in*** to swim with the penguins?

And you dove right in after to save him!
Still holding the ice cream cones!

I think we're getting closer to earlier today... yes, there I am!
Let's see if I can get my attention...

Tachyon *nudge!*
ZZZZT

Whoa! What was *that?*
Huh. It almost felt like time-traveling tachyons... anyway, good night!
Rats! My plan's not working. All I can do is give myself tachyon *goosebumps.*
Get the cake, Benjamin! Get the cake!

Well, if you can't *remake* the past, maybe you should concentrate on *making* the future.
What do you mean?
Our memories are wonderful, but what if you just focused on making *new* ones with the kids?

You're absolutely correct. Heading back...to the present!

It's too bad this invention didn't work the way you wanted.
It's probably for the best. Messing with the time stream can get, well, ***messy.***

Where's the cake?! Is it back here?
Jayden, I hate to admit it, but--

You forgot my cake, didn't you?
I did, and I'm sorry. I'll do my best not to forget again. But for now, let's have some fun!

Best birthday ***ever!***
Love you, Dad!
Love you
too, buddy!

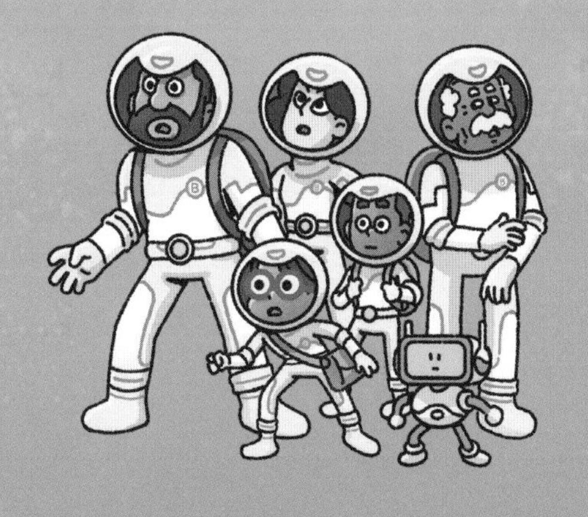

LOOK FOR THESE BOOKS FROM

AVAILABLE **NOW!**

TO READ MORE, VISIT

getepic.com